W9-AQG-366

Originally published as *Zaza en het potje* in Belgium and the Netherlands by Clavis Uitgeverij, 2008
English translation from the Dutch by Clavis Publishing Inc., New York

Visit us on the Web at www.clavis-publishing.com.

A Potty for Zaza written and illustrated by Mylo Freeman

ISBN 978-1-60537-567-0

This book was printed in July 2020 at Wai Man Book Binding (China) Ltd.
Flat A, 9/F., Phase 1, Kwun Tong Industrial Centre, 472-484 Kwun Tong Road, Kwun Tong, Kowloon, H.K.

First Edition
10 9 8 7 6 5 4 3 2 1

MYLO FREEMAN

A Potty for Zaza

NEW YORK

“Look what I have,” Mommy says.
“It’s a potty.”
What a funny thing that is!
Zaza has never seen anything like it.

"Do you know who it is for?" Mommy asks.
Zaza shakes her head.
She has no idea.

Is the potty for Rosie?
No, Rosie is too small for the potty!

Is it for George Giraffe?
No, George is too tall for the potty.

How about Bobby?
Oof, Bobby is much too big for the potty!

The potty can't be for Mo, either.
Mo is way too long for the potty.

How about Mommy?
Zaza has to laugh. Silly!

Who is left?
Zaza sits down on it, and . . . she is just the right size.
It's a potty for Zaza!